White Horse

Yan Ge

Illustrated by James Nunn

Translated from the Chinese by
Nicky Harman

HOPEROAD

First published by HopeRoad 2014

This edition published 2019

P O Box 55544, Exhibition Road London SW7 2DB

www.hoperoadpublishing.com
Twitter: @hoperoadpublish

A CIP catalogue record for this book is available from the British
Library.

ISBN 978-1-908446-98-5
eISBN 978-1-9164671-3-2

Supported using public funding by
**ARTS COUNCIL
ENGLAND**

Printed and bound in Great Britain by Clays Ltd, Elcograf S.p.A.

To Yang Yang

'*White Horse* mesmerizes from page one as events unfold through the unassuming lenses of a child's mind. In recounting how young Yun Yun is trying to make sense of real-life experiences in an adult world, author Yan Ge weaves a fascinating tale of receptive hearts, rebellious spirits and hidden secrets infused with cultural values in this small Chinese community.'

Dunia Magazine

My cousin Zhang Qing and I may not have been the prettiest girls in our small town, but we certainly thought we were. One day, while my aunt was out, the pair of us sneaked into her room and pulled all her scarves out of the drawer. Then we stripped down to our vests, wound the scarves around our heads and shoulders, and stood gawping at ourselves in the mirror.

'Hey, why are we such good-lookers?' said Qing.

'We're the best-looking in the whole world,' I said.

'So who wins out of us two?' Qing asked.

I gave her a long look, then said reluctantly, 'You're prettier than me.'

My cousin pulled the scarf down a bit, décolleté-style, so you could see her collarbone. She had soft budding breasts and turned

sideways on to the mirror, sticking her chest out so she could admire her figure. I gazed at her breasts enviously, because I had nothing. We carried on messing around, rifling through the drawers again and finding my aunt's lipstick. It was the kind that coloured up when it was on your lips. We smeared it on and waited and waited, then my cousin said, 'It only goes red in the sunshine.'

Still swathed in scarves, we went out onto the balcony to sun ourselves but it was still early in the year and chilly. (Of course, neither of us would have admitted that to the other.) We stood there like a couple of hungry nestlings, pouting our lips at the sun and waiting for them to turn bright red.

After a bit, my cousin's face reddened with the cold and she sneezed violently.

Somehow, my aunt always knew what we had been up to when she left us alone. This occasion was no exception. Qing got a beating. That prettiest face in the world was soon running with tears and snot, and no longer quite so pretty. My aunt thrashed her daughter from the sitting room to the bedroom and from the bedroom to the sitting room, while my cousin cried so hard that I felt my heart breaking for her. I stood by the front door, not daring to move, bawling my eyes out.

Then my aunt had to go and start the dinner. When I heard her tearing the spinach, I sneaked into the bedroom, where my cousin lay sprawled limp and exhausted on the bed. She had no more tears left to cry and sobbed soundlessly.

'I'm so envious of you for not having a mother!' she said fiercely.

I did not know how to comfort her. I just sat beside her on the bed, patting the hem of her jacket and said, 'Honestly, it's quite nice to have a mum.'

My aunt always enjoyed taking me to school. The nights I stayed over, she carried my school bag and we were out of the door before 7.30 in the morning. We went through the South Gate market and my aunt always had plenty of people to exchange greetings with: 'Hello Chen, fish for dinner today, is it?' 'Mr Zhu, are you having water spinach again?' 'Doing good business today, Mrs Li?' 'Hello, Mrs Cai!' they greeted her politely. 'Taking your niece to school?'

My aunt always puffed herself up and retorted angrily, 'What do you mean, my niece? This is my daughter.'

After this happened quite a few times, the market shoppers got the message. Now they called to her: 'Good morning, Mrs Cai! You and your daughter are off to school early.'

That made my aunt happy. She gave a loud, clear response and made me call a greeting, too.

One day, after we had gone through the old city gate, my aunt took me by the hand and said suddenly, 'Yun Yun, I really am your mum. Don't you ever forget that.'

'I won't,' I promised.

'If anything's wrong, you just tell me. So long as I'm here, I'll make sure no one ever pushes you around,' she declared.

'Yes,' I said.

That afternoon after school and after much

searching, I found my father in the compound of the old people's home where we lived. He was hemmed in by a bunch of old men who were watching him play chess. As I squeezed through, my dad banged the horse down on the board, taking his opponent's chariot and shouting in elation, 'See my "White horse bright hooves"!'

'Come and cook dinner, Dad,' I said, but he wasn't listening. 'You played like a fool today, didn't you, old Chen,' he said.

He finally realized I was there: 'Yun Yun! You home from school?' Affectionately, he sat me on his knee, holding me firm with one arm, while with the other he carried on playing chess.

I'd been watching chess for so long that every move my dad made I could name: 'Gunfire blasts the mountain' or 'Horse walks into the slanting sun' or simply 'Checkmate!' When it was checkmate, we could go home for dinner.

Mostly, it was noodles for dinner. My dad threw a handful of noodles into the water, and when they were cooked he took a ladleful for himself, gave me a bowlful, and added soy sauce or lard. Then he took a bowl of cooked, minced meat from the cupboard and put a big spoonful on top and we sat there together and gulped down our dinner.

My dad slurped his noodles down, breathing heavily and had finished in less than a minute. He threw the ladle into the sink, wiped his mouth and said to me, 'Yun Yun, wash the dishes, right?'

'Right,' I said.

And before I knew it, he was out of the house and I could hear him next door: 'Mr Zhong, come and have a game of chess!'

I did the dishes and then my homework, or the other way round, or maybe I just did the dishes and, instead of my homework, I stole one of my dad's martial arts novels. Or I shut the house up and dropped in on the neighbours. The old folks always made me welcome. As soon as they saw me coming, they looked out titbits for me: a couple of slices of boiled pork in garlic sauce, or a White Rabbit milk candy left over at the bottom of a tin.

Mrs Yu, who lived at the opposite end of the compound, had the most spending money – ten yuan a month – and sometimes she even gave me a bit of chewing gum, a rarity in those days. On the other hand, Mr Zhong, who lived in our row of houses, was very poor. He habitually went around in a khaki military greatcoat, a hand-me-down from my dad.

Wherever I was, I was free to please myself until nine o'clock at night, by which time all the old folks were asleep, except Mr Zhong and my dad, who were still locked in combat at the chess board. I could go to bed, or not, as I chose, either in Dad's bed or in my own small bunk bed, and so long as I slept, no one cared whether I lay on my back or my side or my stomach. Except for my cousin who warned, 'You should never sleep on your stomach.'

'Why not?'

'You'll squash your chest and your breasts will never grow.'

I was alarmed. I took a look at the small swellings on her chest, and back at my own chest, flat and skinny as pork ribs, and swore to myself that I'd never sleep on my tummy again. It's not too late, I thought. They're sure to grow sometime.

It was summer by then, and when I slept at my cousin's we shared her sleeping mat of bamboo slats and just wore our knickers. We played at being a pair of lovers. My cousin, with those small breasts of hers, was the woman, so that left me being the man. We cuddled up affectionately, and she rested her head in a womanly way in the crook of my neck. I, like a man, put my arm round her shoulders.

'Kiss me,' Qing said. So I did. She pointed to her breasts. 'Kiss me there.'

I was startled. 'How can I kiss you there?'

'But couples always do that,' she said confidently.

So I kissed her delicate nipples. They were tiny, and slid from between my lips, like two cold, boiled peas left over from my dinner.

After I'd kissed them for a while, Qing felt she

9

owed me something in return. 'Shall I kiss you?' she offered.

'Sure.'

So, always fair, Qing kissed my nipples just the way I'd kissed hers. Her lips were wet.

'What do couples kiss like this for?' I asked.

'You're too young to understand,' she said between kisses.

We were growing up quickly and, after the summer holidays, Qing started sixth grade and I went into third grade. 'You shouldn't spend so much time over at her house, now she's working for her middle school entrance exams,' Dad said to me. But I went over there anyway, in any spare time I had, because they had a 21-inch colour TV. Once we'd watched the Flower Fairy cartoons, Qing would start to dress me up: she tied my hair up in a red scarf, and wound a long yellow scarf around my neck. Finally, she put rouge on my lips and cheeks. Then I helped fix her up and we sat on the balcony where we could see the sports field of the middle school next door. Every evening, it was full of young people taking a stroll, some of them in couples.

'This time next year, when I'm in middle school, I'll have a boyfriend, too.'

'You'll be too young to be in love,' I objected.

'Humans only live to love,' she said.

I felt an odd tightening in my chest at her words. Sitting close together, my hand in hers, my hair tied up in a red scarf, I suddenly saw a white shadow moving to and fro on the field. I peered at it: it was a white horse.

'There's a white horse over there,' I said to Qing.

'Where?'

I pointed. 'There!'

'I can't see it.'

A cold shiver ran through both of us.

'You know what I heard?' Qing said. 'If you tie a red scarf round your head, you'll see a ghost.'

With shrieks of alarm, we pulled the scarves off our heads and rushed back into the sitting room.

'Zhang Qing!' shouted my aunt crossly from

the kitchen. 'What's all that noise? Are you crazy?'

She had a shout loud enough to reach all around the house, but she quietened down when my uncle came home. He taught chemistry at the middle school next door and always brought with him a thick pile of exercise books to correct. No one dared make a noise after that. Qing and I sat in her room doing our homework like good girls, until we heard my aunt call, 'Dinner time!' Then we washed our hands and sat nicely at the table, waiting for my uncle to arrive before we helped ourselves to those morsels of stewed duck we'd been eyeing from the moment we came into the room.

After dinner, my aunt went back into the kitchen to do the washing-up while my uncle tested us on our homework. Qing was no good at maths and was always getting told off by her father: 'You've done that sum wrong again. And I told you last time how to do it.'

Then he turned to me. 'Pu Yun, you see if you can do it.'

I came closer, looked at the problem and worked it out. 'Is it 32?'

'Did you see that?' Uncle said to Qing. 'Pu Yun listens to what I teach you, and she can do it. Why don't you try a bit harder?'

Qing glared angrily at me. Every time this happened, she must have thought that surely this time I wouldn't show her up, but every time I did.

When my father came to pick me up around nine o'clock, my aunt bustled out of the kitchen, her hands full of bags of food she had cooked for us to take home. But if Qing was in a bad mood, she would come rushing out and knock the soy milk buns from her mother's hands. 'Don't you give them those! What makes them think they can come round all the time and eat our food?' This enraged my aunt and brought my uncle rushing out of the sitting room. When he bundled Qing into her room, I knew she was really in trouble.

The day after one of these rows, I went to the sixth-grade classroom when school was over. Sure enough, there was a big black bruise on Qing's arm.

I stood in the doorway and called, 'Zhang Qing!'

She ignored me and carried on packing her bag.

But then she came out and, hand in hand, like the best of friends, we went off together to buy a packet of crackers and munched them all the way home.

'Come and have dinner in my house,' said Qing, 'and we can put on make-up.'

That was the day when we finally found some proper lipstick in my aunt's drawer, not one that went coloured after you put it on but real lipstick in a bright scarlet. We stood together in front of the mirror, and Qing said, 'Hey, I can't wait to grow up!'

She put on a pair of glasses and looked at me in the mirror, her lips red as blood.

I responded loyally, 'Qing, you're really pretty.'

Qing flicked her hair back and glanced sideways at me. 'Just wait till I grow up.'

And as the months went by, she did just that. She never waited for me, either.

*

One day I bumped into her in the street. She was wearing a patterned skirt with a white belt. The skirt was in a gauzy material, and with the light shining through it I could see the flowers on her knickers. She was walking down Imperial Culture Alley, looking as thick as thieves with two students, a girl and a boy. My school bag on my back, I stopped and shouted, 'Qing! Qing!'

She ignored me.

'Zhang Qing!' I called again, so loudly the whole street must have heard.

Finally, she turned and looked at me. 'Have you finished school?' she asked.

'Yup.'

'We're off to have some fun,' she said. 'Bye bye.'

'Who's that, then?' asked the boy with her.

'My little cousin. She's still in primary.'

And they went off, laughing, leaving me to carry on at primary school.

I still went to my aunt's house. I was lucky to have my aunt, now that I'd lost my cousin. Qing

was taking evening classes and my uncle was teaching so my aunt and I used to eat dinner together, sitting beside each other at the table. My aunt loved twice-cooked pork. Any time she served this, she had two more bowls of rice, then added some water and the remaining oil and ate it all up.

As she smacked her lips over the pork and rice, she asked me, 'Yun Yun, what's your dad been doing? Why does he never come to dinner here?'

'He's always out with Mrs Xiang the teacher,' I answered.

'Which Mrs Xiang?'

'I think she's his girlfriend.'

My aunt put another melting morsel of fatty pork in my bowl. 'So he's got a girlfriend?' she asked.

'Dad says Mrs Xiang's going to knit me a jumper,' I informed her.

'Knit you a jumper?' my aunt looked con-temptuous. 'And what gives her the right to knit you jumpers? She's not family. You belong to this family. I'll knit you a jumper.'

And she did. It was purple, and my aunt struggled over it as the wool kept breaking. She finally finished it and made me put it on. It hung loose on my skinny frame but she looked at it with satisfaction. 'Very nice,' she said. 'You can wear it till you're grown up.'

It was high summer and too hot for jumpers but I had to keep it on, even though I was sure it was the cause of my prickly heat rash. I looked mournfully at my reflection in the mirror. The face of a young boy looked back at me.

It didn't take long for the news of my dad's new girlfriend to get around town, and when it did, he didn't show his face at my aunt's house to collect me. My aunt was attending an evening study group now and she used to come home with my cousin. One evening, I was sitting watching their TV. 'Yun Yun!' cried Qing affectionately as she came into the room.

'Hello, Qing,' I greeted her. But she went straight into her room and banged the door shut.

As I sat there, my aunt came out and asked my uncle, 'Why don't you take Yun Yun home if you're not in a hurry to get to bed?'

He gave me a ride home on the back of his huge bicycle, through the old town's South Street and then along the second ring road in the direction of West Street until, far in the distance, we could see the lights of the old people's home compound halfway down Xin Street. My uncle left me at the top of the street.

'Mind how you go now, Yun Yun,' he said as he pedalled off.

'Yes, Uncle.'

As I walked the last stretch, my heart was in my mouth. The street was completely deserted and the metal gate to the compound was locked. When I let myself in, old Mr Sun, the gatekeeper, took a look through the window, then went back to his *Old Folks' Digest*. He always had to wait until evening for the paper to make its rounds of the courtyard and finally end up with him.

My dad and I lived furthest from the gate, and I made my way through the pitch darkness.

Even Mr Zhong was asleep in his lonely bed. It was very quiet and the smell of the old folks' canteen dinner hung sharp in the air: pork slices with wood ear mushrooms, Mother Ma's beancurd, fish-fragrant aubergine. The room next door to the canteen was the Supplies Office, where my dad worked during the day, but he had been home for hours by now, sitting reading with Mrs Xiang by the light of the lamp.

She saw me come in and stood up. 'Yun Yun's back. I'd better be off.' My dad took her back to wherever it was she lived.

Meantime, I got into bed, cuddling my new purple jumper in my arms.

Just then, I really missed my auntie.

During a PE lesson at school, Chen Zinian, one of the kids who always got bad marks, said to me, 'Pu Yun, you're still wearing your dirty tracksuit.'

'Mind your own damned business,' I retorted, piling up the sand in the sand-box.

'That's rude.'

He thought 'Mind your own damned

business' was rude? I looked at his hair, parted into neat strands. 'Motherfucker,' I said.

Chen Zinian looked appalled. He jumped up and shouted, 'I'm telling the teacher what you said!'

'Go on, you do that.' I glared, and flung a handful of sand at his oh-so-clean white shirt.

He took a step back and then charged and knocked me into the sand-box. 'You're bad!' he shouted. 'You've got no mum! You've been badly brought up!'

'Motherfucker! Motherfucker!' I flung sand as hard as I could in his face.

There was a big fuss and the teacher took us to the school office, where we waited for our parents to pick us up.

My aunt was the first to arrive, rushing in furiously. 'What's up? Yun Yun? Who's been bullying you?'

I looked at her and burst into tears.

Auntie turned to Ms Zhu, our class teacher. 'Who's been bullying Pu Yun?'

Before Ms Zhu had a chance to open

her mouth, Chen Zinian's father came in. Immediately he saw Auntie, he greeted her politely: 'Mrs Cai, how are you?'

Auntie glowered at him, and said nothing.

'Ms Zhu, what's Chen Zinian done?' Chen Zinian's father sounded worried now.

'The pair of them had a fight in the sports hall,' she said. 'I don't know why.'

'A fight?' Auntie raised her eyebrows. 'Yun Yun, did he hit you?'

Tears pouring down my face, I played my trump card: 'He said I didn't have a mum.'

My auntie instantly leapt up and, seizing the boy by the ear, told him off.

'You're a very bad boy! Such a wicked thing to say! You think you can bully Yun Yun because she has no mum? Let me tell you something. I'm her mum now.'

She was weeping as much as I was, so loudly you would think it was her who had been hit. Her cheeks streamed with tears but she just gave them a quick wipe with her hand, and grabbed Chen Zinian's dad's grey checked jacket.

'You're our neighbour, Mr Chen, you've known Yun Yun since she was a baby. How could you teach the kid to say such wicked things!'

Chen Zinian's dad was scarlet in the face. He wrenched his jacket free of Auntie's grip and retorted, 'Mrs Cai, I've never said anything like that to him. I don't know where the wretch picked it up from.' And he gave his son a smack across the head with his free hand.

Chen Zinian burst into howls of tears.

My auntie led me away. She was hiccupping with sobs, and her eyes were red-rimmed and swollen.

'Don't be angry, Auntie,' I said. 'I'll be a good student from now on and they won't dare tease me.'

'What a good girl you are, Yun Yun,' she said.

But she was still in a temper, and took me to see my dad so she could give him a piece of her mind, too.

My dad hung his head, and didn't utter a word. 'Pu Changshuo,' she began, 'I don't care if you have a girlfriend, and it's none of my business who she is, but you can't neglect your daughter. Either look after her properly or stop being her father and that'll be that. And that Xiang woman's a teacher, too! She should be helping you look after her. Are you completely hard-hearted?'

She went on and on for ten minutes, and only stopped when she remembered we hadn't had lunch. We went to a restaurant to eat. After she left, my dad took me back to school and bought me a lollipop on the way.

'I'm sorry, Yun Yun, I haven't treated you right,' he said. 'I'll be a good dad from now on.'

The only thing I was unhappy about in those days was that Qing felt she was too grown-up to play with me any more. I used to wait at my aunt's house for her to come home from school, but she would shut herself in her room. I don't know what she was doing, but Auntie used to shout to her from the kitchen, 'Zhang Qing! Come out and play with Yun Yun!'

'I'm doing my homework.'

There was nothing Auntie could say to that, so she called me in and said she'd play with me instead.

But Auntie was no fun to play with so I went back to watching TV and eating jam-filled biscuits which she brought back from the food store where she worked.

I knew Qing was keeping something from me. Once, at dinner, I asked her, 'Is it fun at middle school?'

'There's a lot of homework,' she answered, deadpan. 'It's tiring.'

'I can help,' I offered.

She glared at me. 'Do you think this is still primary school? How could you possibly do middle school homework?'

When she'd finished, she wanted to go out with her friends, but my auntie said, 'It's dark. What are you going out for now?'

'We're preparing for the biology class experiment tomorrow,' said my cousin, and she ran out.

I'd never been to biology class; we just had

nature study. While my auntie did the washing-up, I messed around in my cousin's room. I took everything out of her school bag to have a look.

There was an English textbook with some writing I couldn't understand, a pencil case with rubber bands in all different colours, and 70 cents in coins.

I decided to take 10 cents and a red rubber band, because she'd hurt me. A little while later, I found her letters.

The letters were in the lining of her school bag, and as soon as I looked I knew they were love letters. One began: 'Dear Qing . . .'

My heart went pitter-patter and I strained my ears for any noise outside. But my cousin was still out and my auntie was in the kitchen. She called to ask if I wanted an apple, and I said, no thanks. Once I'd read one letter, there was another, half-finished, which was her reply: 'Dear Feng,' it began.

My cousin was in love.

By the time she returned, I had put everything back, even the coin and the rubber band. I was still in her room and she asked warily, 'Yun Yun, what are you doing?'

'Just reading,' I held up my book innocently. She came over and picked up her school bag.

'Did you move this?' she looked suspicious.

'No.'

'Just you leave my school bag alone,' she said severely.

'OK,' I said.

My cousin and her boyfriend had said they'd 'meet after school by the sports ground parallel bars'.

So I went and leaned over the balcony hoping to catch a glimpse of him. I saw my cousin casting suspicious glances up at the balcony, but she didn't see me. My uncle's beloved orchid plants were so bushy, I could duck down behind them.

From up there, I had a panoramic view of the goings-on between the girls and boys at the Pingle Town middle school, which made me feel omniscient and omnipotent. At the start, I only had eyes for my pretty cousin in her corduroy trousers and apricot-coloured top, hanging around the parallel bars. Then the boy turned up. He was taller than Qing, with a bristly haircut and a white shirt. They looked embarrassed, but after a while drew closer, then started strolling around.

After that, they met regularly at the sports ground. Sometimes they went round twice, sometimes five times, and sometimes were only halfway round before they secretly entwined hands. Sometimes there were too many people and even after five circuits they hadn't managed to hold hands. On those occasions, I got bored and began to look at the others. Behind the platform, there was a place where people used to meet and smoke. Sometimes there were quarrels, and once I thought I saw a couple with their arms round each other, kissing on the mouth.

They really were kissing on the mouth, because their arms were round each other and their heads side-on to each other, like in the films. Engrossed, I leaned right over to gape at them. When I pulled myself together, my cousin had gone, and my mouth was full of cold air.

Qing came home and asked my auntie:

'Where's Pu Yun?'

'Doing her homework in your bedroom.'

She came in, looking like a thundercloud: 'You're so crafty!' she said. I realized she must have seen me. 'I won't tell anyone,' I said.

The way she looked at me, I thought she was going to give me a slap, but she just said, 'You're not allowed to tell the grown-ups, otherwise I'll never speak to you ever again.'

I knew we were back together again when she told me his name was Ye Feng, and his parents had jobs in the county town Labour Department. Then she said, 'We're going out together on Sunday, and you can come too.'

At dinner, she told her parents, 'On Sunday, I'm going out with Yun Yun.'

'You spend all day out wandering around,' grumbled my uncle. 'It'll be your final exams soon.'

'Ai-ya,' protested my auntie. 'Let them go out and have a bit of fun. Just don't be late back,' she told us.

*

When Sunday came, my cousin and her boy-friend strolled by the river, with me bringing up the rear. They were hand in hand. After we'd been twice up and down the riverbank, I'd had enough. 'Qing, I can't walk any more,' I called.

'Then stay here and wait for us,' she said.

I sat on the riverbank and they disappeared. I knew they must be sitting somewhere out of sight, kissing. I threw a stone, then another, then I picked up a really big one and smashed it down into Bright Creek as hard as I could.

It was getting dark when I started to call my cousin. 'Qing! Qing! Zhang Qing! Zhang Qing!' Up and down the riverbank I went but she still didn't appear.

I seemed to see something in the eucalyptus trees on the other side, and screamed even louder: 'Zhang Qing! Zhang Qing!' The thing emerged from the trees. It was a white horse.

I burst into tears.

Eventually the two of them turned up and Ye Feng brought me a bag of fruit candies.

'What are you crying for?' said my cousin. 'If

you keep on crying, I won't take you out again.'

She took my hand and we went home. Her boyfriend followed behind and slipped away when we got to the crossroads. She and I walked through the market by the old South Gate, just as close as could be, and I asked her, 'Did you kiss on the mouth?'

'No, of course not,' she said.

'You did!'

'Don't you go telling any grown-ups.'

'Is it nice?' I asked.

'Oh, yes,' she said, finally giving me a direct answer.

When we got home, my auntie asked, 'Did you have fun with your cousin, Yun Yun?'

'Yes,' I said.

One evening, I asked my dad: 'Do you kiss Mrs Xiang on the mouth?'

'What a disgraceful thing to say! Wherever did you get that from?'

'It's on TV,' I said.

'Don't believe everything you see on TV,' my dad said. 'Only dirty foreigners kiss on the

33

mouth. Chinese people don't.'

'Qing, Dad says kissing on the mouth is dirty,' I told her.

She leapt up, grabbed me by the neck and dug icy-cold fingers into me. 'What did you tell your dad?' she demanded.

'Nothing! I just asked if he kisses his girlfriend.'

She released me, flopped back into the chair and said with a smile, 'If he says they don't, I don't believe it.'

'Do Auntie and Uncle?'

She hesitated and frowned. 'Of course not. They're so old!'

We sat together, contemplating the hair-raising thought of my auntie's rude-swearing mouth stuck to Uncle's. 'They can't have done after I was born,' said my cousin firmly.

After a while, she went on, 'My mum's such a bitch; what made my dad decide to marry her?' She was writing back to Ye Feng as she spoke.

'Don't talk about Auntie like that,' I said.

My cousin had a know-it-all look.

'She's a bitch. Everyone in the South Gate neighbourhood knows it.'

I took a long good look at my auntie that evening at dinner. Her eyes were enormous, though now she had big bags under them. She had a small frame, which made her look rather plump. I guessed that before the swathe of brown spots crept up her face, she must have had delicate white skin like her daughter's.

Auntie didn't notice me scrutinizing her, she was engrossed in chewing a morsel of meat. When everyone had finished, she would help herself to the bit she loved best, a bowlful of rice with the meat oil poured over it. I could not help sighing to myself.

'Where did you learn to sigh like that, Yun Yun?' asked my uncle.

My cousin pursed her lips and smiled at me. She was probably imagining those two greasy mouths kissing.

That night, when I got home, I asked my dad again, 'Was Auntie pretty when she was young?'

'Why are you asking that?'

'I think she must have been pretty when she was young,' I said.

Dad smiled. 'She was as pretty as a picture. Every one of us South Gate lads was after your auntie.'

'So who was prettier, Auntie, or Mrs Xiang?'

He looked down, then his gaze focused on the top of my head, then it slid off and landed somewhere else. 'You're too clever for your own good,' he said. 'Don't ask so many questions about grown-up things.'

My dad, my auntie and my cousin all seemed to think I was just a baby. They'd be shocked if they knew how mature I really was. I decided to make friends with Chen Zinian and, in maths class, I gave him my exercise book to copy. I got 92 per cent and he got 95 per cent, and the teacher praised both of us and said we made good desk-mates.

'Why did you get three more marks more than me?' I asked him.

'Because you got the last sum wrong!'

'You're crafty,' I said coldly.

In PE class, Chen Zinian came over: 'Pu Yun, at the next maths exam . . .'

'I'll give you mine to copy from,' I said.

His eyes lit up. 'Thank you. You're so nice. I'll take you to have some jerky.'

'I don't want you to.'

'Then just tell me what you want,' he said.

'Kiss me on the mouth, right?'

Chen Zinian's mouth dropped open. He took a step back and blurted out, 'You've got a dirty mind!'

We had another fight.

Auntie said to me, 'Zhang Qing has gone so strange recently. She's off out every evening. Do you know what's up with her, Yun Yun?'

'No,' I said.

Auntie sliced the sausage and looked at me suspiciously. I used to think she knew everything about the pair of us but she seemed to have got duller in the last few years. She turned her gaze back to the sausage, and popped a slice speckled with fat into her mouth, and then one in mine, too.

My cousin came in. 'Hey! Are you two cooking sausage for dinner? I want some!' she cried excitedly.

She was wearing a red down-filled jacket, blue jeans (the height of fashion) and almost-new trainers, and she bounced and bobbed into the kitchen, grabbed two slices of sausage and stuffed them into her mouth.

My auntie swallowed and aimed a slap at her daughter: 'Zhang Qing! Greedy pig, don't stuff your mouth like that.'

'I'm hungry,' said my cousin, with a grin which showed a mouthful of half-chewed red and white sausage.

I tried to shoot Qing a warning glance but she wouldn't look at me.

Sure enough, my auntie asked her, 'Where have you been? You've been running around a lot these last few days.'

'I've been studying, just studying,' my cousin said.

'Nonsense!' My auntie piled the sausage slices in a bowl, sneaking another slice as she did so.

'You think I don't know you? You haven't been studying.'

'I have. I really have!' Finally my cousin looked at me. All of a sudden she looked less cocksure.

'You just behave yourself,' my auntie said fiercely to her, and carried on getting the dinner ready.

'I really was studying!' my cousin wailed.

'Well, next time, you take Yun Yun with you, and don't leave her kicking around all on her own in the house.' And my auntie buried her head in the cupboard, looking for the pot of braising sauce.

'Take *her*!' My cousin launched into a furious argument with her mother, but glared at me so fiercely that it might have been me she was quarrelling with.

Dinner was braised chicken wings, thighs and claws – special dishes for New Year's Eve. My dad was coming, and bringing Mrs Xiang with him.

'Have some chicken claws, Xiang,' Auntie

offered her.

'She doesn't like chicken claws,' my dad said. 'Give them to me; I like them.' He swiped them from Mrs Xiang's bowl and passed her a chicken thigh with his chopsticks instead.

'Huh!' my auntie said, annoyed. 'You've always liked those chicken claws.'

'It's nothing to do with you, what Changshuo likes to eat,' said my uncle.

'Who are you to say what's my business and what isn't?' retorted my auntie.

'You're always sticking your nose in,' said my uncle. 'It doesn't matter who likes the claws and who doesn't.'

'You know nothing about anything,' said my auntie.

'Oh yes I do. I know very well.' And my uncle pushed his chair back from the table.

I don't know what Qing was thinking, but this was the first time I'd heard Uncle and Auntie having an argument. Uncle stalked off into their room and slammed the door.

Auntie looked stunned. She forced a smile at

Mrs Xiang, then burst into tears.

The three of us soon made our escape. My cousin, looking pitiful, saw us out.

'I'm sorry, Xiang,' my dad said to his girlfriend. 'We didn't put on a very good performance today.'

'It doesn't matter,' said Mrs Xiang. 'Everyone around South Gate knows about what happened between you and her.'

My dad squeezed her hand and said solemnly: 'That was a long time ago. It's all water under the bridge.'

I suddenly thought of something very philosophical: The world is full of secrets…

It certainly was.

Even I realized we'd be spending a lot more time on our own now. Mrs Xiang didn't come as often, and my dad spent all his time playing chess with old Zhong. I learnt to cook noodles and my dad instructed me, 'Keep an eye on the water in the pot, and when you can see little bubbles coming to the surface, put the noodles in, a bundle as

thick as five of your thumbs.'

When the noodles were cooked, I took my dad a big bowlful and one for old Zhong, too. My dad said I should stir in two soupspoons of lard for him and half a spoonful for old Zhong.

'What a good girl you've got there,' the old man said cheerfully. My dad was deprecating:

'No she's not. She's a complete nuisance!'

After a while, I went and collected the bowls and they set to again, with a clattering of pieces on the chessboard.

One day, on my way back to the flat, I noticed a bright red banner hanging on the entrance

gate, inscribed, 'The Old People's Home extends a big welcome to the County National People's Congress leader.'

I was bored these days so I looked forward to his visit. 'Will it be long before the CNPC leader comes?' I asked.

'He'll be here in the next few days.'

The great man turned up on the seventh day of the New Year. He arrived with his driver in a small minibus. The old folks from the compound all took their stools to the canteen to welcome him, and my dad went, too. I hung around in the doorway, waiting for the meeting to be over. There was burst after burst of applause from inside, and speeches from the CNPC man, from the Director of the Home, from representatives of the old folks themselves, then another speech from the great man.

No one else spoke after his final speech and the Director shouted from the platform, 'Let's give our leader a big hand!' The applause was so thunderous it drowned the snoring of some of the old gents, but not the banshee-like wail that suddenly caught my ears: 'Yun Yun! Have you seen Zhang Qing?'

I felt a cold shiver, and turned to see my auntie approaching. She did not look at all pretty today, in fact she looked downright ugly. Her hair stuck out all over her head and her eyes were swollen with crying. Grabbing my arm, she said, 'Yun Yun, have you seen your cousin?'

She pushed her face up close to mine. I hadn't seen her for a while and I had forgotten how old she looked. Completely different from those photographs of them when they were young that I'd seen in the family album. 'No, I haven't,' I finally remembered to reply.

'Ai-ya! Ai-ya!' she wailed.

'What's happened to Qing Qing?' asked my dad. He had come out before the VIPs and now pulled Auntie and me to one side.

'She's run away from home!' My auntie's face was drenched in tears, but at least she managed to avoid wiping the mess on my dad's jacket.

They went off to look for my cousin. My heart was thumping with fear, but they didn't want me to go with them. 'You stay at home, girlie,' said my dad. 'If your cousin comes back, don't let her go out again.'

I trotted back and forth, from our home to the entrance gate and back again. The old folks, men and women alike, realized something was going on and strolled around the compound looking smug. When they met me, they asked, 'Where are you off to in such a hurry, Yun Yun?'

Anxiously, I told them, 'My cousin's run away from home!'

The second time, they asked me, 'Yun Yun, have you found your cousin yet?'

'No,' I answered even more anxiously.

'Don't worry,' they reassured me, 'she'll turn up!'

Eventually it got dark. The smell of beef and potato strew wafted from the canteen, and everyone went over to fetch their dinner in enamel bowls. But my dad and my auntie didn't come home.

Finally I went out into the street to see if I could see them. It was a cold, dark night, and my hands were like two blocks of ice. I walked out of the alley, as far as New South Gate Street. I didn't see a single person I knew. It was as if the familiar neighbourhood had simply disappeared and the streetlights looked far, far away.

I walked and walked, looking for my cousin, my dad and my auntie, or any familiar face.

I began to cry. The more I cried, the colder I got. Passers-by asked me, 'What's up, kid?'

'My cousin's disappeared,' I said anxiously.

I thought I saw a white horse emerging from Jin Jia Alley, followed by a twittering crowd of school students, but they swept by me and my cousin wasn't among them.

When I at last got back to the compound, I was exhausted from crying.

There was a light on in the flat and I started to run. My dad and my auntie were standing in my doorway. I could see their dark figures tightly embraced, just like in foreign films.

After a while, they pulled apart but stood close together. I crept closer. My auntie saw me first. She pounced on me with a cry of 'Yun Yun! Where have you been? We've been looking everywhere for you.'

My dad came out of the doorway and told me off. 'Didn't I tell you to guard the house?'

The way they looked made me think I must have imagined their kissing. 'What about my cousin?' I asked.

'She's back, she's gone to sleep,' said my auntie.

I rushed inside and saw Qing asleep in my dad's bed. She had been crying, her face was covered in red blotches and her hair was in a mess, but she still looked like an angel, with those long, long eyelashes resting on her cheeks.

We shared the same bed that night, and Qing's body seemed to give off a sort of fragrance.

When school began again, my aunt and my dad took my cousin and me to see Qing's new teacher, the Mrs Xiang we all knew. My auntie was laden down with bags, which she deposited with a clatter on the teacher's desk.

'Mrs Cai, you really shouldn't have brought all these presents, you're too kind, I don't know what to say!' said Mrs Xiang.

'Oh, it's nothing,' said my auntie. 'At New Year we all got so much food given us at work, far too much for us to eat. Please don't think anything of it.' I sat on the sofa watching this exchange of civilities, itching for them to hurry up and sit down and open the boxes of sweets, so I could have some of my favourite peanut toffees. My cousin sat woodenly beside me. The purpling bruises and scabs on her face, where my auntie had dug her fingers in, were still visible.

Finally they sat down and Mrs Xiang opened the sweets. 'Yun Yun, Zhang Qing, come and have some.'

As I hurried over to take some sweeties, I heard my auntie say to the teacher, 'I hope Zhang Qing won't be any trouble in your class this term.'

'No trouble at all,' said Mrs Xiang. 'Zhang Qing's such a good girl.' She reached over and stroked my cousin's face. Qing didn't protest but her face was expressionless.

My auntie pulled the teacher's hand away and clasped it affectionately in her own: 'She's not good at all,' she said. 'Her dad and I have been so angry with her.'

'All kids makes mistakes,' said Mrs Xiang. 'But they can mend their ways.'

My auntie gave a despairing sigh. 'If only she would! But she goes around from morning till night, looking like the devil's got into her. Anyway, if she cheeks you, you have my permission to give her a beating.'

I was still chewing my sweetie when my cousin stood up and pointed to my auntie. 'What mistakes did I make? I didn't make any mistakes.

And no one has the right to give me a beating.'

My auntie's mouth gaped as if she'd swallowed a duck egg. Then she quickly pulled herself together and launched herself at her daughter, digging her fingers into Qing's face and yelling, 'You bad girl! Flunking out of school and playing around with boys at your age! And I only had a couple of words with you and you ran away from home. How can you say you never made a mistake? Are you going to mend your ways? Are you?'

My cousin in her turn dug her sharp fingernails into my auntie's hand and shrieked back, 'It's not illegal to have a boyfriend! What's wrong with having a boyfriend?'

My dad rushed over to pull them apart but my auntie dealt him a swift blow and redoubled her efforts to subdue her daughter. 'Bad girl!' she ground out between gritted teeth. 'I just can't keep you under control.'

Mrs Xiang appeared rooted to her chair with terror as the battle raged. I carried on eating sweets and tried to reassure her. 'It's nothing,

51

Miss, nothing at all.'

The words were hardly out of my mouth when my cousin swept all her mother's gifts off the teacher's desk onto the floor, which brought a stinging slap in response. Trembling with rage, my auntie yelled at her, 'You slut! So young and such a slut! Playing around with a boy like that!'

My cousin slumped to the floor, just like one of those beautiful but ill-starred girls on the TV. She turned her face up to her mother, her eyes filled with tears, but what she said was, 'I'm not as much of a slut as you.'

My auntie threw herself on her: 'Who are you calling a slut?'

The pair wrestled on the floor, squashing a tangerine which had rolled out of the gift bag. The muddy blood-red juice went all over the back of Qing's green windcheater, looking like fresh poo.

In the space of a few days, my cousin seemed to have grown as shrewish and quarrelsome as her mother.

The teacher hesitantly got to her feet and

reached out to them: 'Please don't fight! Don't fight!' but her words were drowned by the accusations the combatants were hurling at each other.

Finally it was my dad who pulled my auntie to her feet, looking the way he did when he was about to spank my behind. 'Cai Xinrong, have you gone mad? Why are you beating her?'

It looked as if my auntie was going to have another swipe at him, but suddenly she crumpled and seemed to get smaller. My cousin lay on the floor, crying as if her heart would break. There was no room on the floor for my auntie so she threw herself weeping at my dad instead. My dad patted her back. 'It's all right, it's all right, stop crying, stop crying now. What a scene you're making!'

At this point, I thought it was time for me to put in a word. I got to my feet and said, 'Stop crying. Stop crying.' Mrs Xiang stood behind me and echoed my words: 'Stop crying. Stop crying.'

We really didn't know which one of them we were trying to comfort.

*

These days, I went to old Mrs Yu's house to do my homework after school. The weather gradually got warmer and Mrs Yu used to sit in her doorway on a rattan chair reading a book. I carried my stool out and sat beside her, using another stool as a table to do my homework on.

On this particular day, my teacher had taught us a new phrase and we had to copy it out five times. The phrase was 'crystal clear'. I had done it three times when Mrs Yu asked me: 'How old are you, Yun Yun?'

'Ten years and three months,' I said.

The old woman gave deep sigh. 'Is it really ten years?'

'Yes,' I said.

'Time's gone by in the blink of an eye,' she said.

'Yes, it has,' I said.

'Your mum was still in the land of the living then . . .'

I copied 'crystal clear' for a fourth time, then a fifth.

When I finished my homework, I went to the

canteen with Mrs Yu for my dinner. All the old folks were really nice to me. Whenever they saw me, they beamed. 'What a good girl you are, Yun Yun, are you coming for your dinner?' Zhu the cook, who was ladling out the portions, asked me, 'Which is your favourite, Yun Yun? I'll give you a bit extra.'

I stood on tiptoe and took a long look at the food. Then I announced, 'I want that stuff.'

The cook laughed and said, 'That's not "stuff", Yun Yun, that's Gong Bao chicken.' And he gave me an extra-big ladleful.

We all sat around a big table eating our dinner. Everyone found something to say to me: 'What classes did you have today, Yun Yun?' 'You'll be in fifth grade soon, won't you, Yun Yun?' 'You got the best marks, didn't you, Yun Yun? When you get into university, old Mr Sun will give you a big red envelope,' and 'Such a grown-up girl; you're getting prettier by the day.'

I finished my dinner, and sat watching the old folks finishing theirs. Then Mr Zhu, the cook, came out of the kitchen and handed me another full bowl to take home. 'This is for your dad,' he said.

A sudden silence fell, and I felt the eyes of everyone on me as I left, carrying the bowl. Outside in the fresh air, I managed to avoid the other residents in the courtyard and the pitying looks they gave me. I opened my front door, and smelled alcohol fumes. 'I'm home, Dad,' I said.

My dad was sitting slumped on the sofa, looking rather sinister in the half-dark. But he knew it was me and grunted, then took the bowl and began to eat. He even remembered to ask me, 'Yun Yun, did you work hard at school today?'

'Yes,' I said.

He gulped his food down, sniffing as he did so. 'I'll wash the bowl,' I said.

He said, dejectedly, 'No, I'll wash it.'

I went back to Mrs Yu's to fetch my school bag, and she said, 'Why don't you sleep here tonight, Yun Yun?'

'I'm going home,' I said.

'Is your dad all right?' she asked cautiously.

'He's fine.'

'Such a pity,' she sighed as she showed me to the door. 'Such a pity. And all because of a woman.'

As I made my way home, I wondered if the woman she was referring to was my auntie or Mrs Xiang, the teacher.

It was my auntie who turned up that evening.

As I opened the door, I saw her in the sitting room, clearing liquor bottles and cigarette butts off the coffee table. 'Hello, Auntie,' I said.

'Oh, you're back, Yun Yun,' she said, in an odd tone.

She was crying without making any noise. I looked at her helplessly.

Finally I said, 'Are you ill, Auntie?'

'No,' she said, tearing off a piece of toilet paper to wipe her nose.

'You should go home,' my dad told her. 'I'll clear up.'

Auntie ignored him.

'You really should go,' he repeated. 'If you're late home, Zhang Xinmin will get annoyed.'

Auntie was still bent over the table, wiping up the cigarette ash. She scrubbed her nose again, this time without toilet paper, just pinching it between her thumb and forefinger. Then she flicked her fingers.

The room was very dim and I couldn't see where Auntie's snot landed, but I heard her say in a hoarse voice, 'He doesn't want to do it with me any more.'

'Don't talk rubbish,' said my dad heartily. 'You should make him feel a bit special, he's been good to you.'

'Huh! None of you know what you're talking about.' Auntie's voice shook.

Dad sighed. 'I've let Xiang down, and you, too.'

'It's nothing to do with who let who down, it's just life,' my auntie said gently. Then she blew her nose on her fingers again, flicked her fingers, and the snot landed somewhere beyond the margins of the lamplight.

The next day, she came to meet me after school. I didn't see her at first, because there was the usual noisy crowd around the school entrance. Then I heard her shrill call: 'Yun Yun!' and spotted her by the flowerbed, waving at me. She was smartly dressed today, and really stood out from the rest of the women.

'Auntie!' I cried in delight, and threw my arms around her.

'Hello, sweetie.' Auntie hugged me back, equally delighted.

She bought me some spicy pickled turnip and I tucked into it, getting chilli oil all round my mouth. Auntie gave me some paper hankies from her bag. 'Wipe your mouth, Yun Yun,' she said.

'Have some, Auntie.' I offered her the bag.

'No, thanks, you finish it,' she said with a big smile. So I did.

We got to my cousin's middle school and Auntie held my hand as we waited for Qing to come out. The bell went, and the middle school students burst through the doors like jungle beasts. I couldn't see my cousin among them but Auntie spotted her and shouted loudly, 'Zhang Qing!'

My cousin was standing with her boyfriend, Ye Feng. Auntie rushed over to her with me following, but Qing grabbed Ye Feng by the hand.

This was a standoff: Auntie and me, Qing and Ye Feng. The bystanders drew back.

My cousin's face darkened. 'Why have you brought Pu Yun?' she asked. 'And where did you go last night?'

'Where are you taking this young man off to?'

Ye Feng tried to free his hand but failed because Qing had a tight grip on it. 'We're boyfriend and girlfriend,' she pronounced to her mother.

Auntie let go of my hand and gave my cousin a slap on the face. 'You slut!' she shrieked. I knew a fight was imminent and hurriedly stepped back, but Ye Feng stood rooted to the spot as my cousin hawked and spat a gob of saliva that landed on Auntie's front.

'You're the slut! If I'm a slut, where do you think I learned it from?'

Auntie went pale. She went to tug her daughter's hand from Ye Feng's,shouting, 'You bad girl! Come back home with me right now.'

I stood at the school gate, as passers-by craned their necks to see what was going on. I was terrified that Mrs Xiang might finish her class and come out and see. Luckily, Auntie finally succeeded in getting hold of my cousin's hand and, by the force of her plump body, pulled her away. Then she turned to Ye Feng and snarled, 'Are you really Zhang Qing's boyfriend?'

'No,' said Ye Feng, who had gone as white as a girl. 'No,' he repeated, 'we're not boyfriend and girlfriend.'

My cousin's frenzied shriek nearly made me throw up my turnip pickle.

We finally got home. As we went up the stairs Qing stumbled twice and my auntie got a firm grip on her. I was too scared to be anywhere near her and followed Auntie into the kitchen. Auntie mixed some honey in water and gave me the cup. 'Go and give it to your cousin.'

I took it to Qing's room. She was wailing and

swearing at the same time, though I don't know who at. I went over and said, 'Qing, drink some honey water.'

I hadn't actually handed it to her but she took it anyway. She sipped, realized she was thirsty, and gulped the rest down. The first thing she said when she'd finished was: 'That double-crossing creep, Ye Feng! He'd better not think I want anything to do with him ever again.'

Uncle didn't come home for lunch so we three had lunch without him. Auntie made a point of selecting a nice morsel of meat from the stewed beef and potato dish to put into her daughter's bowl.

Then my cousin said, 'I don't want to go to school this afternoon.'

'Of course you've got to go to school,' said Auntie.

Qing's head jerked up and she looked at us. Her eyes were bloodshot, the lids swollen into two slits. 'How can I go to school looking like this?' she said.

Auntie was startled into silence. Then she

said, 'All right, you can study by yourself in your room.'

We both missed school that afternoon. We went to her room, and my cousin got Ye Feng's letters out of her drawer, then took her time cutting them to ribbons, one by one.

I watched her wield the scissors. 'Would you like some help?' I offered.

She said quietly, 'It's fine, I'll do it. You go and watch TV.'

So I did, but secretly I regretted not going to school because there was nothing much on TV on Tuesday afternoons. As I flicked through the channels with the remote, I could hear my cousin: she had a bit of a cry, then fell silent, then cried again, then fell silent, then had another howl . . .

Finally, she was quiet.

We were good friends for quite a long time after that, maybe because our last falling-out had been so painful. Auntie came to fetch me from school in the afternoon, we went together to collect Qing, then back home. My uncle sometimes stayed in the office, and sometimes got home before us after doing the shopping on the way. My cousin and I sat at either end of the coffee table, bent over our homework, while my auntie and uncle busied themselves in the kitchen getting the meal ready.

My cousin had lost weight, which made her eyes look enormous in her thin face. If she finished her homework first, she would sharpen my pencils for me. She upended my pencil case and worked on them one by one, until they were as sharp as weapons. 'Why do you do your homework in pencil?' she asked me.

'The teacher says I can,' I said.

The next day in class, Chen Zinian took out a new 'Hero' fountain pen, gold-coloured, and waved it in front of my face.

'Have you seen my new pen?' he said. 'It cost more than 50 kuai.'

I looked daggers at him and carried on writing my notes with my pencil.

That day, dinner was at our home. There

was fish stew with pickled vegetables, stir-fried Chinese cabbage, stewed pig's tail and a salad of sliced pig's ear.

I told my dad, right there in front of my auntie: 'Dad, I want a fountain pen.'

'I think I've got an extra one,' he said. 'You can have it.' He went to the drawer, got out the fountain pen and gave it to me. It was a black plastic one.

'Buy me a Hero fountain pen, Dad,' I said. 'Chen Zinian's got one.'

'Are they expensive?' he asked.

'A bit over 50 kuai, I think,' I said.

'Are you crazy?' he said.

'Oh, for heaven's sake, I'll buy you one, Yun Yun,' said my auntie.

'No, you're not to; it'll get her into bad habits,' said my dad.

We carried on eating silently. When my auntie was about to leave, my dad said, 'Take some back for Zhang Xinmin.'

'Of course,' said Auntie. And they searched the house for the biggest enamel bowl, and my

dad filled it to the brim with the fish stew.

My aunt and my cousin left, and my dad went into the kitchen to wash up. He took ages over it, then suddenly rushed white-faced out of the house.

'Dad! Dad!' I shouted after him.

He ignored me.

I waited for him to come back, slowly finishing the dishes. Finally, he arrived with Auntie, her face tear-stained, and my cousin Qing following silently behind.

I looked at them, and Dad said, 'Qing Qing, thank you.'

Qing Qing patted Dad on the shoulder just as if she was his sister.

That evening, Qing Qing and I shared my bed. It was appallingly quiet in the house.

Neither of us slept. I felt fear clawing at me.

I asked Qing, 'What's up with them?'

'They're boyfriend and girlfriend,' she said. I said nothing.

My cousin was quiet for a while, then said, 'That's love.' Everything in the world seemed to change at her words.

I must have dropped off because I was woken up by a banging noise, which echoed through the empty courtyard. 'What's that?' said my cousin, clutching my hand in alarm.

'It's old Mr Zhu next door, stacking up his coal briquettes with the tongs.'

Another silence, then we heard panting coming from Dad's room. It sounded inhuman, like some monster was lurking in there.

Now it was my turn to take fright. 'What's that?' I asked my cousin.

But she was asleep by then, her palms wet with sweat. My heart was pounding in fear, and I daren't let go of her hand. I strained my eyes into the darkness and waited for the monster to come for us once it had eaten up Dad and Auntie.

I could see a corner of the courtyard through the window. Unlike our room, it was in complete blackness, then a patch of it paled to dark blue, then white, and a white horse emerged silently.

Suddenly Qing dug her fingers into my hand. So she was awake after all. 'Qing, did you hear that noise?' I burst out.

She grunted. It sounded more like a groan than an answer.

I had become a girl with a secret. As I gave my maths exercise book to Chen Zinian to copy, I heaved a deep sigh. 'What's up?' he asked.

I sighed again. 'You wouldn't understand.'

He said stupidly, 'I understand I shouldn't be copying from you.'

He finished copying and gave me the exercise book back, stroking my hand as he did so.

His touch felt like it went all the way up my arm. It kind of hurt. 'What are you doing?' I asked.

'Nothing.'

But it had happened and I knew things had

69

changed between us. At lunchtime that day, he was waiting for me at the school entrance. I walked over to him. 'Let's go and eat wonton,' he said.

'OK,' I said.

We walked along with the other pupils to get our dumplings, and Chen Zinian said, 'Pu Yun, I shouldn't have said you don't have a mother that time.'

'It's OK,' I said. 'I don't have one.'

He said very gently: 'You've still got me.'

My heart skipped at his words, and I knew this was love.

I thought and thought about this and finally decided to tell Qing. 'I've got a boyfriend,' I said.

'Who is it?' she asked

'Chen Zinian, a boy in my class.'

She smiled. 'What a pair! You're both as young as each other.' I didn't like her contemptuous attitude one bit.

'It's true!' I said.

'Right, right.'

We carried on with our homework. Then

Auntie came in. 'Where are the scissors, Yun Yun?' she asked.

'Aren't they in the drawer?'

She found them and went back to the kitchen.

'You're just a pair of babies. You don't know what you're talking about!' whispered my cousin, when she'd gone.

I gave her a lofty look. 'I know you've kissed on the mouth.'

She smiled. 'Kissing's nothing.'

I looked at her. 'Are you and Ye Feng back together again?' I asked.

'Why would I get back with an immature kid like that?' she said.

During the next morning's class, I took a long look at Chen Zinian. He'd grown into a good-looking boy, better-looking than Ye Feng, I reckoned. We sat at the same desk and held hands. After a while, he put his hand on my thigh and rubbed it back and forth. It made me ache all over. I looked at him, and he looked back at me. I remembered my cousin's words: 'Kissing's nothing.'

The class carried on and I said to him, 'Let me use your pen for a bit?' He let me try it. It was heavy. It made me feel very grown-up when I wrote with it. But at the end of the class, he said, 'Give it back, I'm off home now.' So I had to give it back to him.

When school was finished and I went back home, I met old Mrs Yu as I went into the compound. She gave me a slightly unfriendly look, and I wondered guiltily if she knew I'd had my thigh felt by a boy.

'Mrs Yu!' I called anxiously. But she ignored me.

'Mrs Yu!' I called again.

Finally she turned to look at me. 'Yun Yun, is your dad back?'

'I don't know.'

'You tell your dad he's done enough harm.'

The look she gave me was scary, and I rushed off home.

I didn't tell my dad what Mrs Yu had said, because I was trying to figure out how to persuade him to let Auntie buy me a fountain pen. After all, they were boyfriend and girlfriend now, so couldn't she buy me a really good pen?

At dinnertime, Auntie and Qing were there. Then Uncle came and knocked at the door.

Auntie refused to open up. He knocked and knocked.

The four of us – me, my dad, my auntie and my cousin – all sat there watching as he peered through the window, then went back to the door to knock again.

Finally my dad said, 'Go and open the door, Pu Yun.'

'Zhang Qing, you go and open it,' said Auntie.

Qing and I went hand-in-hand to open the door. 'Hello, Dad,' said my cousin.

Uncle came in, white-faced, holding a teacup between finger and thumb. 'Cai Xinrong, you have no sense of shame!'

'It's nothing to do with you,' said Auntie.

Uncle turned to Dad. 'Pu Changshuo, you're shameless, too. You both are. I'm the only decent one here.'

Dad said nothing.

'I know you're together,' said Uncle. 'The whole neighbourhood knows you're together, and I've had to swallow that. You've really done the dirty on me.'

No one said anything. Auntie opened her mouth but no sound came out. 'You really did the dirty on me, pretending you were related. You thought you could get away with it because I wasn't from around here. Cai Xinrong, do you really think I don't know why you split with him and married me instead? You really think I don't know, don't you? You reckon I just saw how pretty you were, and the bit of money your family had, and you thought you could make a fool of me. You slept with him all that time ago and did me out of what should have been mine. And you're a brute, Pu Changshuo. You couldn't keep your hands off my woman, could you? You really made a fool of me.'

'Don't go talking rubbish about things you know nothing about,' said my auntie.

'What don't I know? I know everything, I know that you two are a bad lot, I know he knocked up a crazy woman in the old people's home, and that's why you two split. Do you really think I didn't know that?'

They all started yelling then, and I started crying. Qing sat on the sofa with me, she was crying, too. I shouted at them, 'Dad! Auntie! Uncle!'

Qing yelled: 'Dad! Mum!'

But the three of them paid no attention to us. Finally, Uncle flung the contents of the teacup all over Dad.

Auntie shrieked and tried to pull Dad back but it was too late. Dad rolled around on the floor, screaming. White smoke eddied up from the puddle of liquid.

Uncle just stood there, saying over and over, like an alarm clock, 'You both did the dirty on me. You both did the dirty on me.'

Old Mr Zhu sat with me by my dad's hospital bedside all night. The old man sighed and cried until his eyes went all gummy.

I asked him, 'Mr Zhu, will Dad die?'

'No, he won't die,' he said. 'But he'll never be

any good again.'

'You mean he won't be able to walk?'

'Yes, he'll be able to walk, but he'll never be any good.'

Tears poured down his face. I could see my dad's hands and feet were fine, but I cried, too.

My cousin came a few times. She didn't dare come in so I went out. 'Qing,' I said.

She gave me a Thermos. 'Mum said to give it to you both.'

I said nothing. Old Mr Zhu came out and pushed her away. 'Be off with you. This is all the fault of that wretched mother of yours. Go on, scram!'

Qing went, though she cast a pitiful glance back.

I moved in with Mrs Yu. She and old Mr Zhu spent all day sighing over me, which I found unbearable, so in the evening I went out and walked down the main road. I got all the way to my auntie's house, but I didn't dare go in. Their compound was even less well lit than ours. I stood at the entrance. I saw white horses coming out. I counted them as they passed me: one, two, three, four, five.

One of the horses looked like my auntie and I followed it down the road until we got to South Gate market. Inside, the market was completely deserted and enveloped in inky darkness. It was slippery underfoot, too. We walked around it once, then a figure rushed past me, shouting loudly. I didn't understand but I fled anyway. I ran and ran until I was exhausted.

It was old Mr Zhu who found me. He carried me back to the old people's home, his face tear-stained and his whiskers prickling my face. 'Poor child, poor child,' he kept saying. I wanted to tell him that his whiskers were prickling me and I didn't like it, but he looked so stricken that I said nothing.

Mr Zhu, Mrs Yu and all the other old folks took over my care. I didn't go to school and I had no friends to play with. Every day I ate with them, listened to the state radio broadcasts, practised taiqi and slept when they slept. A very long time passed and finally my dad came home.

Once he was back, I could go back to school, but a pupil who'd transferred from another school was in my place at my old desk. None of my classmates talked to me, and even Chen Zinian shunned me, the ungrateful wretch. I didn't talk to my new desk-mate, either.

At the end-of-term exams, I did well but lost my place at the top of the class to my new desk-mate. That made me even less willing to talk to him.

One day, my auntie secretly came to meet me after class. She kept hugging me and crying. 'Yun Yun, why don't you speak? Why don't you say anything?' She looked terrible when she cried like that, and I didn't say anything to her.

After a few minutes, some of the teachers came out and pulled her off me, and took me home.

I don't know how many times my dad broke down in tears and cried in front of me. It really started to annoy me. He begged my pardon, said he hadn't brought me up right, he'd let my mum down, let my auntie down, let my cousin down.

'I'm so sorry, Yun Yun,' he said. 'I promised your mum I'd give you a good upbringing, and treat you just like you were my own child. I'm so sorry, I've let you down.

'I've let your auntie down too,' he went on. 'All these years, I never told her properly what happened back then, and she just rushed into marrying Zhang Xinmin, and he's off his head. He beats her up, too.'

He bawled some more, then he said, 'I've let Qing Qing down too, and you know what's happened? She's left home, she's dropped out of school, and she's having to fend for herself. I'm so sorry about that.'

He cried so much it gave me a headache. I pulled out a bit of toilet paper from under the pillow and gave it to him. 'Don't cry,' I said.

Dad gave a start of surprise and hugged me, exclaiming, 'Yun Yun! You're talking again!'

I had a flash of inspiration and said, 'Dad, buy me a fountain pen. A Hero one.'

'Yes, yes, of course I will,' Dad said.

I shared Dad's bed that night. Around

midnight, a white horse came in. It looked at me, then went out again. I gave my dad a shove and woke him up. He mumbled, 'Who's opened the door?' Then he got up and shut it.

One day I saw my cousin in the street with a boy. Because I still wasn't talking much, I didn't shout after her. The boy looked like a real lout, and my cousin had got so fat that she was waddling like a duck. They stopped to buy baozi dumplings and she got into an argument with the stallholder. She started to shout and scream so loudly the whole of South Gate could hear her. Just like my auntie, in fact.

They didn't see me. But I could see that Qing was growing exactly like her mother.

I carried on at school. They really piled the homework on in sixth grade. We had to knuckle down, our teachers told us, because this was our last year in primary school and we had to pass the middle school entrance exams. They were all very kind to us, and when my dad saw me off to school, he told me these last few days were the 'sprint finish' and to keep my nerves steady, not to get anxious, and I'd pass into middle school for sure. When he slipped an extra five kuai in coins into my bag, I set off down the street feeling everything was going well. The only problem was that I'd been seeing white horses again, following after people in the street, in ones, and twos, and threes . . .

I got to school and there was a horse in the classroom. It was standing in front of the newspaper board at the back of the room, getting in my way so I couldn't sit in my place. I talked occasionally to my desk-mate nowadays, and I said to him, 'Pull the desk out a bit, there's a horse in the way.'

He looked at me. 'What?'

'Pull the desk out a bit, there's a horse in the way,' I repeated.

He looked at me in amazement. Maybe he didn't understand the local accent. 'What horse?' he said.

'Can't you see it? Beside you.'

He smiled. 'You're making it up.'

I sat down in my place and opened my school bag. 'I'm telling you the truth. Didn't you know my mum had me with a white horse? She told people about it, but they didn't believe her. They said she was crazy. Then they accused my dad of having knocked her up.'

His mouth dropped open. 'You scare me,' he said.

'Lots of people know about it in the town,' I said to him earnestly. 'You can go and ask them.'

He went pale, and I knew I'd scared him good and proper. I didn't say anything more to him.

For a few days after that, he didn't talk to me. In fact he didn't even dare look at me. I reckon he must have heard all about what was going on between our family and Auntie Cai and her family.

A week later, we had our final exams. When we got the results, I had finally regained my place at the top of the class. The teacher was delighted. 'What an intelligent girl you are, Yun Yun, such a good student,' she said.

On the last day of school, I got a new school bag and pencil case as a prize. I could put my shiny new Hero fountain pen in it. And so I graduated from primary school. I was going to start middle school where I could have a boyfriend. Or maybe not . . . I couldn't imagine anyone taking any interest in me.

I went up to the platform with my school bag, to the applause of my classmates. I could see Chen Zinian down there, whey-faced, clapping away, and I could see my desk-mate, too. He was still looking at me as if he'd seen a ghost. Both of them looked so stupid I couldn't help smiling. My cousin used to tell me that smile made me look like a crazy. But no one said that to me any more.

THE END

Acknowledgements

To Qiu Huadong, editor of People's Literature,
for publishing this story in 2008.
To Nicky Harman, my dear friend and
translator.